Henry Van Dyke's

The Other Wise Man

ISBN-13: 978-0-8249-5565-6

Published by Ideals Children's Books
An imprint of Ideals Publications
A Guideposts Company
535 Metroplex Drive, Suite 250
Nashville, Tennessee 37211
www.idealsbooks.com

Printed and bound in Italy by LEGO

Library of Congress Cataloging-in-Publication Data:
Kennedy, Pamela, 1946—
     The other wise man / by Henry Van Dyke ; retold by Pamela Kennedy ; illustrated by Robert
Barrett.
        p.   cm.
   Summary: Journeying with the other Magi to Bethlehem to see the newborn Jesus, a fourth Wise
Man delays to help others in need but eventually finds his King.
    1. Jesus Christ—Nativity—Juvenile fiction. 2. Magi—Juvenile fiction. 3. Christmas stories. [1.
Jesus Christ—Nativity—Fiction. 2. Magi—Fiction. 3. Christmas—Fiction.] I. Barrett, Robert, 1949-ill.
II. Van Dyke, Henry, 1852-1933. Other wise man. III. Title.
PZ7.K38490t
89-7590
[Fic]—dc19
CIP
                        AC

10 9 8 7 6 5 4 3 2 1

Designed by Marisa Jackson

Henry Van Dyke's

The Other Wise Man

Retold by Pamela Kennedy
Illustrated by Robert Barrett

ideals children's books.
Nashville, Tennessee

In the days when Augustus Caesar was the ruler of many kings—including Herod, who reigned in Jerusalem—there lived among the mountains of Persia a certain man named Artaban.

Artaban was one of the Magi, men who study the heavens in search of truth about God. He and three of his friends from far away had discovered in the ancient writings a promise that at a special time a beautiful new star would rise in the eastern sky. At the rising of that perfect star, a great King would be born. He would be the Truth sent from the One God—the Son of the Most High.

Artaban believed the time was very near. He had sold his house and all he owned to buy three jewels to carry as gifts for the newborn King.

Now as the sun began to set, Artaban reached into his colorful silk tunic and brought out the three great gems: a sapphire as blue as the Persian sky at night, a ruby as red as the first rays of sunrise, and a pearl as white and pure as the snow. Artaban held the priceless gems together in his hands and gazed into the darkening sky.

That was when he first saw the tiny spark on the horizon. He watched it grow larger and larger as it rose higher into the sky, with flashes of light surrounding it.

"It is the sign," exclaimed Artaban. "The King is coming and I will go to meet Him!"

Artaban's three friends had said they would wait for him only ten days after sighting the star. He knew he must race to meet them at the Temple of Babylon, or they would leave to seek the King without him.

Quickly saddling Vasda, his fastest horse, Artaban galloped off, barely stopping for food or drink. He rode across brown mountain slopes and level green plains. He picked his way carefully over rocky mountain passes and crossed swirling rivers.

Poor Vasda was exhausted and could hardly walk as night fell on the tenth day. But Artaban urged his horse onward.

Suddenly, Vasda stopped and Artaban saw something in the road. He approached the dark shape for a closer look. It was the body of a man. The man seemed dead, but as Artaban turned to go, the poor man reached out one hand and grasped the hem of the wise man's robe. The man was still alive!

Artaban saw that without help the sick man would not live. If Artaban nursed him, the man would recover quickly. But Artaban would be too late to meet his friends at the Temple. He turned his eyes toward the star he had been following and prayed, "God of Truth and Light, show me the way of wisdom, which only You know."

Artaban turned back to the sick man. He carried the man to the foot of a palm tree. There he gave the poor fellow cool water and a healing potion from the remedies he always carried. For several hours Artaban cared for the man as he slowly regained strength. Finally the man awoke fully and asked, "Who are you?" Artaban told the man of his quest.

"I have nothing to repay you for your kindness," said the man, "but I will tell you this. From our Hebrew prophets we have learned that the Messiah will be born in Bethlehem, not in Jerusalem, and that is where you must seek Him."

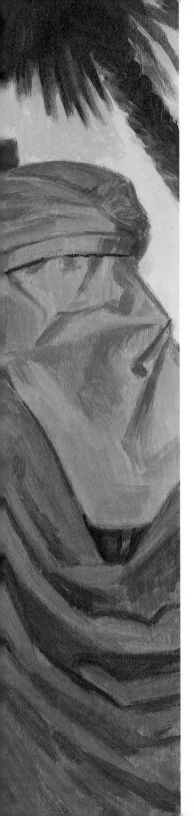

Thanking the man, Artaban galloped off toward the Temple, but the sun's first rays were shining as they entered the grounds. Anxiously Artaban searched for his friends, but they were gone. He found a note which read: "We have waited past midnight and can delay no longer. We go to find the King. Follow us across the desert."

Artaban sat upon the ground in despair. "How can I cross the desert," he cried, "with no food and an exhausted horse? I must return, sell my sapphire, and buy a camel and food for the journey. Only God knows whether I will lose my chance to find the King because I stopped to show kindness."

And so the other wise man sold his precious sapphire, bought a camel and supplies, and set out across the desolate desert.

After many weeks, Artaban arrived in Bethlehem. He came upon a stone cottage; sitting inside was a young woman rocking her baby to sleep. Artaban knocked at the open door, and the woman motioned for him to enter. Artaban told the woman of his three friends and the Baby for whom he searched.

The young mother listened, then nodded, saying, "Yes, there were three strangers from the East who came and gave precious gifts to Joseph and Mary and their newborn Son. But they left suddenly, and just last night Joseph took his little family and disappeared. It is whispered that they have fled to Egypt to escape some unknown danger."

Artaban's heart sank. He had failed once more.

Suddenly, there came the noise of wild confusion and uproar in the street. Women screamed, men cried out, and the clanging of swords and armor filled the air. Artaban ran to the doorway of the cottage as the woman snatched up her baby and hid in the shadows of the room.

"The soldiers! The soldiers of Herod are coming for our children!" The shouts filled the air as a towering centurion approached the tiny cottage. Artaban stood still, filling the doorway, and glared into the soldier's eyes. Then he slowly reached into his tunic and brought out the huge ruby, watching the soldier's face gleam with greed.

"I am all alone here," said Artaban, "and waiting to give this gem to the centurion who will leave me in peace."

Quickly the soldier snatched the jewel, then turned and shouted, "March on! There is no child here."

The soldiers ran on down the street, leaving the other wise man and the grateful mother weak with relief.

"O God of Truth, forgive me for telling this lie and for giving to a man that gift which was to be for You."

The woman spoke softly over her sleeping child. "Because you have saved my little one, may the Lord bless you and keep you all your days."

The next morning Artaban decided to follow the baby King and His family into the land of Egypt. But his task was not an easy one.

Month after month, year after year, the other wise man searched for his King. He traveled to the pyramids and the Sphinx, to the palaces of the Pharaoh and the River Nile. But always the answer was the same: no King was to be found.

Although he did not find anyone to worship, he found many to help. He fed the hungry and bought clothes for the naked. He cared for the sick and visited those in prison. Still he carried the beautiful pearl close to his heart, hoping one day to present it to the One he continued to seek.

After thirty-three years of searching, Artaban had grown very old and tired. But he decided to take one last journey. He thought that perhaps he might find the clue that would at last lead him to the King.

Arriving in Jerusalem, Artaban watched a pushing, shouting crowd in the narrow streets.

"What is this uproar?" he asked a shopkeeper.

"Have you not heard?" the man replied. "Two famous robbers are to be crucified today along with another man called Jesus, who claimed to be the Son of God. He is going to be executed because He said He was King of the Jews."

Artaban's heart raced. Could it be that he had found his King at last? Perhaps if he hurried, he could arrive in time to offer his great pearl to the enemies of the King and rescue Him before He died!

Gathering his robes around him, Artaban hurried up the dusty street. Just before he reached the city gates, he was stopped by a troop of soldiers dragging a young girl whose hair and dress were tangled and torn.

She cried out, "Have pity, kind sir! My father died owing these men a great sum of money. I am to be sold as a slave to pay the debt. Please save me from a life worse than death!"

Artaban was so close to the end of his search for his King—could he give it all up now? Then he looked into the eyes of the helpless girl. One thing was certain—rescuing her would be a true deed of love. And wasn't the ability to love the gift of the One True God?

Artaban placed the pearl in the hand of the weeping girl. "This is your ransom, child," he said. "It is the last of my treasures which were to be given to the King."

At that moment, the sky darkened and echoing peals of thunder rumbled through the hot streets of Jerusalem. The walls of the houses rocked to and fro as the earth rolled like the waves of the sea.

The soldiers fled in terror, leaving Artaban and the girl alone.

Suddenly, a heavy section of roof tile broke loose and crashed down upon the other wise man. As Artaban fell to the ground, he heard a quiet, yet insistent, voice speak to him over the thunder.

"Artaban," the voice called softly, "you have been a good and faithful servant. I was hungry and you fed me. I was naked and you brought me clothes. I was in prison and you visited me. Come now to the rest I have prepared for you."

"Not so, Lord," whispered Artaban with the last of his strength. "When did I do all these things for You?"

And the voice answered, "Whenever you helped one of my people in need, you helped Me."

The peace of understanding fell upon Artaban's soul
like a gentle rain, and he smiled. His journey on earth
was ended. His treasures were accepted.
The other wise man had found the King.